GOAT

HOG

ME

CAT

HORSE

COW

DOG

DUCK

RABBIT

HEN

J

THE GRUMPY MORNING

Pamela Duncan Edwards

ILLUSTRATED BY Darcia Labrosse

SCHOLASTIC INC.

New York Toronto London Auckland Sydney
Mexico City New Delhi Hong Kong

ISBN 0-590-05722-7

Published by Scholastic Inc., 555 Broadway, New York, NY 10012,
by arrangement with Hyperion Books for Children. SCHOLASTIC and
associated logos are trademarks and/or registered trademarks of Scholastic Inc.

12 11 10 9   1 2 3 4/0

Printed in the U.S.A.   14

First Scholastic printing, March 1999

The artwork for each picture is prepared using Schminke watercolors on Papier Special.

This book is set in 20-point Egyptienne Bold.

For James Peter Ellison Lawley—
to celebrate your first birthday,
March 28, 1998
—P. D. E.

For my sister Lérie
—D. L.

I heard a cow begin to moo,
"I need to be milked! I really do."

She mooed at the dog, who began to bark,
"It's time for breakfast. It's no longer dark."

I heard a goat begin to bleat,
"Where are my oats?" and she stamped her feet.

She stamped at the hog, who began to squeal,
"I'm waiting for slop. I'm due for a meal."

I heard a rabbit begin to thump,
"I want my pellets. I'll never grow plump."

He thumped at the horse, who began to neigh,
"I'm hungry. I'm hungry. I'm hungry for hay."

I heard a duck begin to quack,
"What's going on? I must have my snack."

She quacked at the cat, who began to meow,
"I'd like a cuddle. I'd like it now."

I heard a hen begin to cluck,

"My grain is late. That's just my luck."

I saw a moth land on the nose
Of the sleepy farmer, still in a doze.

She opened an eye and said with a cry,
"Is that the time? Oh, my! Oh, my!

"Good morning, cow.
Good morning, dog.
Good morning, goat.
Good morning, hog.

"Good morning, rabbit.
Good morning, horse.
And duck and cat and owl, of course.
Such a **HAPPY** morning, isn't it, hen?"

Then she fed them

And milked them

And loved us,
All ten!

COW

DOG

DUCK

RABBIT

HEN